This is Phonic.

It was a sunny morning.
Bee, Snake, and Inky had gone to the park.

In a corner of Inky's house was Phonic. It was dark in the corner.

Inky, Snake, and Bee ran in.
Inky went to get some drinks.

"Did you see that juggler in the park?" said Snake.

"Yes," said Bee.

"He was fantastic!" exclaimed Inky.

"We did have a splendid morning," said Bee.

"Yes," agreed Snake and Inky.

"Well, I am glad *you* had fun," said Phonic. "I see you did not worry about me. I have been stuck here on this desk," he complained.

"We are sorry, Phonic!" cried Bee. "But you cannot come out with us. You need to be plugged in."

"Yes," agreed Phonic, looking sad.

"Hmmmm... I think I have a plan," muttered Inky, and scampered off.

Soon she was back with a big, flat, black box.

"This is a laptop," she said to Phonic. "Load yourself onto a disk."

Then she loaded Phonic's disk onto the laptop, and...

...there was Phonic, up on the screen!

"Phonic can come with us on our next outing," said Inky.

"Brilliant!" cried Snake and Bee.